illustrated by Harry Bishop

This abridged edition first published in 1985 by
Deans International Publishing
52–54 Southwark Street, London SE1 1UA
A division of The Hamlyn Publishing Group Limited
London · New York · Sydney · Toronto

Text and illustrations this edition
Copyright © Deans International Publishing,
a division of The Hamlyn Publishing Group Limited, 1985

ISBN 0 603 00340 0

Printed and Bound by Purnell and Sons (Book Production) Ltd.
Paulton,
Bristol.
Member of BPCC plc

Illustrated Classics

ROBIN HOOD

Robin Hood

Robin Hood was a gallant outlaw, clad all in Lincoln green, who roamed the forest with his mighty bow, robbing the rich to give to the poor—courteous and dauntless, ever ready for a jest! He was outlawed for breaking laws which the people privately liked to see broken, and all his lawless acts were much juster than the unjust laws. He was the protector of women and of anyone who could not protect himself.

Robin was devout and God-fearing, but he had no use for idle monks and pompous churchmen. He stood out against Prince John, who was oppressing the land while the rightful king was in a foreign prison; but when King Richard himself returned, no subject was more stoutly loyal than Robin Hood.

This brave outlaw was really Robert, Earl of Huntingdon, born at Locksley, near Nottingham, about 1160, in Henry II's reign. His father was one of the last of the Saxon barons, and his mother was a niece of Guy of Warwick and sister to Gamwal of Gamwal Hall. Robin Hood's cousin, William Gamwal, became, later, one of his closest followers (as "Will Scarlet").

After the loss of his parents, home, and lands occurred—sacrificed to the rapacity of Prince John, who usurped the King's place during his absence at the Crusades—Robin saw his castle burnt to the ground by the Normans, who to him were alien robbers. However, he escaped with his life, and fled to Sherwood Forest. There, on the cool grass under a mighty oak, he lay, full of rage, planning vengeance against his enemies. But he loved the forest—the singing birds, the whistling trees, the playful squirrels, the rural scents and sounds, all soothed his troubled spirit. Anger passed and gave place to peaceful calm, and, one with Nature, in the dim evening light of the saddest day in his life, he, an outlaw, fell on his knees and vowed:

"To honour God and the King,
To help the weak and fight the strong,
and to take from the rich and give to the poor."

Robert of Huntingdon thus became "Robin of Sherwood", or, shortly, "Robin Hood."

Those were the days when dense forests covered much of England, when monks ambled along the highways on their ponies and knights rode by on prancing war-steeds, when the poor people told tales at the village merry-making—and when Robin himself and his merry men roamed through the greenwood.

7

Little John

"No sport have we seen for several days," said Robin Hood one bright spring morning, "so I intend to go abroad to seek adventures forthwith. But listen, my merry men, remember well my call. Three blasts upon my horn I will blow in my hour of need; so come quickly, for I shall want your aid."

With a wave of his hand, he set off, and strode along until he came to a narrow bridge that spanned a little stream. At one end of it there stood a man, a good seven feet tall, who carried a staff that looked like a small tree trunk.

"Now, stand back, my good fellow," said Robin, "and let the better man cross first."

"Nay," answered the stranger; "stand back yourself, for I am the better man here."

"That we shall see," said Robin Hood; "for if you dare to move one step forward I will send a good Nottingham shaft between your ribs."

"You prattle like a coward," said the stranger, "to talk of shooting with your bow, when I have only this plain staff to defend myself."

"Faith, never have I had a coward's name in all my life before," replied Robin, and, so saying, he went to the wood and cut himself a stout oak staff, six feet in length. Then, taking their staffs by the middle with the two hands wide apart, Robin and the stranger stepped upon the narrow bridge and gave blow for blow in one of the stoutest quarterstaff bouts that ever man had witnessed.

Robin smote the stranger upon the ribs until his jacket smoked like a damp straw thatch in the sun, and the stranger gave Robin a crack on the crown that caused the blood to flow, and still both kept their footing. But at last the stranger gave Robin such a blow that he fell head over heels into the water.

"And where are you now, good lad?" cried the stranger, roaring with laughter.

Robin laughed too as soon as he could get his breath, and, scrambling to the bank, said:

"I must own you are a brave soul as well as a stout fellow with the quarterstaff, and have fairly won the fight.

"Yes, a fair fight fairly won!" said Robin Hood. Then he set horn to lip and blew a loud blast. Scarcely had the echo died away than his men appeared, a score or two of stout bowmen, all clad in Lincoln green.

"Good master, how is this?" cried Will Stutely, seeing Robin Hood dripping from head to foot.

"This fellow has tumbled me in the brook," replied Robin.

"Then in he shall go too." And the lads made for the stranger, and would have given him a good ducking and also a drubbing, had not Robin cried out, "Stop! He has beaten me in fair fight, and if he will stay with us and be one of our men he is right welcome." So the stranger was accepted.

"What is your name?" Robin asked, as the stranger gave him his hand.

"John Little," answered the stranger solemnly, at which all the men laughed heartily, and Will Stutely cried out:

"Little you are indeed, and small of bone and sinew, and therefore you shall be christened Little John!"

"Then come, my merry men," laughed Robin Hood, "and we will prepare a christening feast for this fair infant."

So through the forest they went until they came to a great oak tree with broad-spreading branches and 'neath it a seat of green moss, where Robin was wont to sit at feast and merry-making with his good men about him. A brace of fat does from the king's fine herd was brought forth, and a barrel of humming ale was broached.

Then, whilst great fires crackled and the savoury smell of roasting venison filled the glade, some of them held contests with the quarterstaff, and others set up garlands on the branches of trees and shot at them in archery practice. When the feast was ready, all sat down, and Robin Hood placed Little John at his right hand.

And thus, amid jest and song and good cheer, they christened Little John, who was to win renown second only to that of Robin Hood himself.

The Great Shooting Match at Nottingham

Now, all this time, the proud Sheriff of Nottingham was trying in vain to bring Robin Hood to justice. So many times had he tried and failed that the king had spoken harsh and scornful words. Then at last he bethought himself how he might use guile to lay his hands on the daring outlaw.

"It is of no avail," thought the Sheriff, "to seek out that evil knave Robin Hood in his woodland haunts. But if I could only persuade him to come to Nottingham Town, I warrant I would capture him."

So he decided to proclaim a great shooting match to which everyone who could draw a longbow should be bidden. An arrow of gold was to be the prize, and he who won it fairly and squarely should be hailed by all as the greatest archer throughout the length and breadth of the land.

When Robin Hood heard of the Sheriff's proclamation, he called his men about him and said:

"Men, I would have one of us win this fair prize that our sweet friend the Sheriff offers, and therefore will we take our bows and shafts and go to Nottingham Town."

"Have a care, good master," said one of the followers. "I have heard it said that this same shooting match is a trap whereby the knavish Sheriff would draw you into the town and capture you."

"Then," said Robin, "we must meet guile with guile. We shall lay aside our suits of Lincoln green and go in disguise—some as shaven friars, some as rustic peasants, and some as tinkers or as beggars. How like you that plan, my merry men!"

"Good, good!" they cried heartily.

Arrival of the Great Day

The great day arrived, and at the appointed time the Sheriff took his place in the seat of honour near the target. The ten best archers were chosen to shoot again.

"Can you see Robin Hood amongst those ten?" asked the Sheriff of a man-at-arms standing near.

"Nay, I cannot, your worship," answered the man. "Six of them I know right well and of the others none is of Robin Hood's size, except, perhaps

a bunch of tall ferns, he espied a man, with a missal book on his lap and a leather bottle at his lips, in the act of drinking. So long the bottle remained tilted in air that Robin stole close ere the other saw him. Robin stood still, and the bottle was slowly lowered, displaying a perfectly round, fat face as red as a cherry, with small, laughing brown eyes fringed with heavy eyebrows. The cheery friar's shaven crown shone like glass, and it too was fringed with a circlet of curly hair. He had a broad fat neck which was quite bare, and at the back of it was a cowl of rough, brown cloth attached to a loose, flowing robe of the same stuff, covering a powerful and strong-limbed body. Round his middle was buckled a leathern belt that held some keys, a string of beads, and a dagger. Beside him on the ground lay a sword, a buckler, and a steel cap.

As he slowly took the bottle from his lips he beheld the stout yeoman standing there, and straightway such a look of amazement came over his funny red face that Robin burst forth into a loud, hearty laugh. "Holy man," said he, "I thought that bottle was glued to your face, so long and lovingly did it cling to those cherry lips. If there is anything left within it, the draught must be right pleasant. I would like some to sweeten my dry throat."

"Ah! would you now?" was the answer. "Then why not test yon cool, sparkling brook from where the bottle was filled?"

"Nay, nay, good Friar, you wouldn't make such pretty gurgling music with water as I heard from you just now. Precious little water hath passed your lips this many a day."

"Well," said the Friar, "a pious man ought not to deny a stranger who asks a drop to quench his thirst." So saying, he passed the bottle to Robin.

Robin took a long pull and found the liquor so good that he tipped the bottle higher and higher, keeping it so long tilted upright that at last the Friar jumped to his feet with a roar like a bull, saying:

"You greedy guts, by Saint Wilfrid I will part your mouth and my bottle with a cuff over your ribs that will land you on the other side of the brook!"

"Ay," said jolly Robin, smacking his lips, "right good Rhenish water, I trow! Thank you for the loan of the bottle, which I will straight away refill from the brook for your future use."

"Nay," cried the Friar, peering anxiously down the neck of the bottle, "be off while there yet is peace between us."

that tattered beggar in scarlet, but he has a beard of brown instead of yellow, and he is blind in one eye."

Each of the ten now shot again, and then from these the three best were chosen for the final contest. One of these was the tattered stranger in scarlet with the patch over one eye; another was Gilbert o' the Red Cap, one of the Sheriff's own archers. Twice they shot, all three, and it was soon seen that the match lay between Gilbert and the tattered stranger. On the third shot Gilbert's shaft lodged close beside the spot that marked the very centre.

"Well done, Gilbert!" cried the Sheriff joyously. "Now, ragged knave, let us see if you can shoot a better shaft than that."

The Ragged Stranger's Shot

All held their breath as the ragged stranger stepped forth. Hitherto he had shot so quickly that one could scarce take breath between the drawing and the shooting, and men marvelled that one blind of one eye could shoot so well. Now he shot with greater care. Straight flew the arrow and so true that it smote a feather from off Gilbert's shaft and lodged in the very centre.

"Here, my good fellow," said the Sheriff. "Take the prize, for well and fairly you have won it. I swear you draw a better bow than that same cowardly Robin Hood, who dared not show his face here today."

That afternoon, in the depths of Sherwood Forest, Robin Hood's men feasted merrily, but the soul of their leader was vexed. "I would like to let the Sheriff know who it was that won the golden arrow from out his hand," said Robin.

Then up spoke Little John: "Let me go to Nottingham Town, and I will send yon Sheriff news of this by a messenger such as he does not expect."

The Sheriff Gets a Surprise

That night, as the Sheriff sat at meat in his great hall, a blunted grey goose shaft with a small scroll attached came through the window and fell upon the table. The Sheriff opened the scroll and grew red with rage, for on it he read:

Now Heaven bless thy grace this day,
    Say all in sweet Sherwood,
For thou didst give the prize away
    To merry Robin Hood.

How Robin Hood Met Friar Tuck

For a time after the winning of the golden arrow, the merry outlaws kept themselves close in Sherwood Forest. When the larder was well supplied with game the great oak glade was given up to sport. Some would play at bowls, or at dice; others would have wrestling matches, bouts at quarterstaff, or mock duels with sword and buckler. But their favourite and never-ending delight was shooting with the long-bow—that trusty weapon which made them so justly famed and feared.

Little John took a bow-string and hung up a dead squirrel from a bough at five hundred feet away, and after taking careful aim, because the wind swayed the mark, he sped his shaft clean through the squirrel's body amid resounding cheers.

"God's blessing on thy head," said Robin. "Gladly would I walk a hundred miles to see one that could match that."

At this Will Scarlet laughed full heartily.

"That is not so hard to do," said he, "for at Rubygill Abbey there dwells a curtal friar that can beat both him and you."

Then Robin leaped up lightly from the green-sward, where he had been lying.

"Now, by'r Lady," exclaimed he, "neither food nor drink will I touch until I have seen this friar of yours, were he in very truth a hundred miles away. Make ready to lead us, while I don my cap of steel, broadsword, and buckler, to meet this holy archer."

"It be no hundred miles, good uncle," said Will. "We shall gain Rubygill Abbey ere noon."

So Little John, Will Scarlet and Robin strode through the forest at a quick gait, mile after mile without a stop, till they came to Needwood Forest hard by Tutbury, where Friar Tuck had in days past received Will Scarlet to his broad bosom, learned to love him, and taught him all his skill with sword, long-bow and quarterstaff.

When the three outlaws were still some way off, they caught sight of the Abbey below them, through a slight opening of the trees.

"There," said Will Scarlet, "you will find the man you want."

"Well," said Robin, "you two remain here, would parley with this man alone."

So saying, he strode forward, leaving Little John and Will behind, till a blast from his bugle should call them. He trudged along till he came to a stream, by the side of which, seated upon the ground, that tattered beggar in scarlet, but he has a beard of brown instead of yellow, and he is blind in one eye."

Each of the ten now shot again, and then from these the three best were chosen for the final contest. One of these was the tattered stranger in scarlet with the patch over one eye; another was Gilbert o' the Red Cap, one of the Sheriff's own archers. Twice they shot, all three, and it was soon seen that the match lay between Gilbert and the tattered stranger. On the third shot Gilbert's shaft lodged close beside the spot that marked the very centre.

"Well done, Gilbert!" cried the Sheriff joyously. "Now, ragged knave, let us see if you can shoot a better shaft than that."

The Ragged Stranger's Shot

All held their breath as the ragged stranger stepped forth. Hitherto he had shot so quickly that one could scarce take breath between the drawing and the shooting, and men marvelled that one blind of one eye could shoot so well. Now he shot with greater care. Straight flew the arrow and so true that it smote a feather from off Gilbert's shaft and lodged in the very centre.

"Here, my good fellow," said the Sheriff. "Take the prize, for well and fairly you have won it. I swear you draw a better bow than that same cowardly Robin Hood, who dared not show his face here today."

That afternoon, in the depths of Sherwood Forest, Robin Hood's men feasted merrily, but the soul of their leader was vexed. "I would like to let the Sheriff know who it was that won the golden arrow from out his hand," said Robin.

Then up spoke Little John: "Let me go to Nottingham Town, and I will send yon Sheriff news of this by a messenger such as he does not expect."

The Sheriff Gets a Surprise

That night, as the Sheriff sat at meat in his great hall, a blunted grey goose shaft with a small scroll attached came through the window and fell upon the table. The Sheriff opened the scroll and grew red with rage, for on it he read:

> Now Heaven bless thy grace this day,
>   Say all in sweet Sherwood,
> For thou didst give the prize away
>   To merry Robin Hood.

How Robin Hood Met Friar Tuck

For a time after the winning of the golden arrow, the merry outlaws kept themselves close in Sherwood Forest. When the larder was well supplied with game the great oak glade was given up to sport. Some would play at bowls, or at dice; others would have wrestling matches, bouts at quarterstaff, or mock duels with sword and buckler. But their favourite and never-ending delight was shooting with the long-bow—that trusty weapon which made them so justly famed and feared.

Little John took a bow-string and hung up a dead squirrel from a bough at five hundred feet away, and after taking careful aim, because the wind swayed the mark, he sped his shaft clean through the squirrel's body amid resounding cheers.

"God's blessing on thy head," said Robin. "Gladly would I walk a hundred miles to see one that could match that."

At this Will Scarlet laughed full heartily.

"That is not so hard to do," said he, "for at Rubygill Abbey there dwells a curtal friar that can beat both him and you."

Then Robin leaped up lightly from the green-sward, where he had been lying.

"Now, by'r Lady," exclaimed he, "neither food nor drink will I touch until I have seen this friar of yours, were he in very truth a hundred miles away. Make ready to lead us, while I don my cap of steel, broadsword, and buckler, to meet this holy archer."

"It be no hundred miles, good uncle," said Will. "We shall gain Rubygill Abbey ere noon."

So Little John, Will Scarlet and Robin strode through the forest at a quick gait, mile after mile without a stop, till they came to Needwood Forest, hard by Tutbury, where Friar Tuck had in days past received Will Scarlet to his broad bosom, learned to love him, and taught him all his skill with sword and long-bow and quarterstaff.

When the three outlaws were still some way off they caught sight of the Abbey below them, through a slight opening of the trees.

"There," said Will Scarlet, "you will find the holy man you want."

"Well," said Robin, "you two remain here. I would parley with this man alone."

So saying, he strode forward, leaving Little John and Will behind, till a blast from his bugle should call them. He trudged along till he came to a brook, by the side of which, seated upon the ground among

a bunch of tall ferns, he espied a man, with a missal book on his lap and a leather bottle at his lips, in the act of drinking. So long the bottle remained tilted in air that Robin stole close ere the other saw him. Robin stood still, and the bottle was slowly lowered, displaying a perfectly round, fat face as red as a cherry, with small, laughing brown eyes fringed with heavy eyebrows. The cheery friar's shaven crown shone like glass, and it too was fringed with a circlet of curly hair. He had a broad fat neck which was **quite bare, and at the back of it was a cowl of rough,** brown cloth attached to a loose, flowing robe of the same stuff, covering a powerful and strong-limbed body. Round his middle was buckled a leathern belt that held some keys, a string of beads, and a dagger. Beside him on the ground lay a sword, a buckler, and a steel cap.

As he slowly took the bottle from his lips he beheld the stout yeoman standing there, and straightway such a look of amazement came over his funny red face that Robin burst forth into a loud, hearty laugh. "Holy man," said he, "I thought that bottle was glued to your face, so long and lovingly did it cling to those cherry lips. If there is anything left within it, the draught must be right pleasant. I would like some to sweeten my dry throat."

"Ah! would you now?" was the answer. "Then why not test yon cool, sparkling brook from where the bottle was filled?"

"Nay, nay, good Friar, you wouldn't make such pretty gurgling music with water as I heard from you just now. Precious little water hath passed your lips this many a day."

"Well," said the Friar, "a pious man ought not to deny a stranger who asks a drop to quench his thirst." So saying, he passed the bottle to Robin.

Robin took a long pull and found the liquor so good that he tipped the bottle higher and higher, keeping it so long tilted upright that at last the Friar jumped to his feet with a roar like a bull, saying:

"You greedy guts, by Saint Wilfrid I will part your mouth and my bottle with a cuff over your ribs that will land you on the other side of the brook!"

"Ay," said jolly Robin, smacking his lips, "right good Rhenish water, I trow! Thank you for the loan of the bottle, which I will straight away refill from the brook for your future use."

"Nay," cried the Friar, peering anxiously down the neck of the bottle, "be off while there yet is peace between us."

"Do you know," asked Robin, "of a certain curtal friar in these parts named Tuck?"

"Maybe I do, and maybe I do not. If you mean him of Rubygill Abbey, the place is but a few rods down the glade when you've crossed the brook."

"Ay, truly," said Robin, "but I see no place to cross without wetting my new hose. I pray you, therefore, kind and good Friar, carry me across on those broad shoulders. Come, tuck up your robe and bend your back that I may meet this same curtal friar in seemly fashion."

Then the Friar closed one eye, screwed up his mouth, and placed his finger upon his brow as in deep thought. At last he said: "What—if the good Saint Christopher were so willing, my unworthy self should not refuse." So saying, he laid down his missal and, tucking up his skirts, took Robin Hood on his back. He plunged into the flowing water up to

his waist, carefully feeling his way over the pebbles on the bottom, and spake no word, good or bad, until he reached the further bank.

Then Robin leaped lightly from his back and set off briskly for Rubygill Abbey.

"Hold! Not so fast, my fine fellow!" cried the Friar. "For now I think I have left my missal and my steel cap upon the other side."

"Well," said Robin, "There is nothing to stop you going back to get them."

"Nay, but," said the Friar smiling, "one good turn deserves another, and therefore you must carry me back on your shoulders, for with another ducking I may take a chill or fall sick of divers pains and rheums."

"What if I should not?" said Robin.

"Then I will baste your hide with your own sword which I carried safely over and now hold."

Now Robin did not like the thought of playing pack-horse to this burly Friar. But he thought that the fellow spake truly enough concerning the sword, so he bent his back, with no very good grace. Straightway the Friar began to prod his heels into Robin's sides to make him go the faster, though he had to go slowly and carefully over the rough bottom with so weighty a burden. But he spoke no word, and after much floundering and splashing they reached the bank in safety, where the Friar got his steel cap and his buckler.

"Now," said Robin, panting and sweating with his hard work, "it's my turn, and you shall carry me back, or I will put a shaft through your fat body as easily as a maid skewers a capon."

"Why, so I will," said the Friar. "So put up your bow, and come along, for it is ill to shoot a holy man that has done you a service."

So Robin once more mounted the broad back of the lusty Friar, and, becoming jubilant, shouted, "Come up, gee, woa!" rapping with his heels the stout Friar's shins, who quietly plodded along, without a word, toward the middle of the brook. But of a sudden he gave a mighty heave of his shoulders, and Robin flew right over his head into the brook with a loud splash, while the Friar stood holding his broad ribs from bursting with laughter.

"Now my fine fellow," he cried, "choose whether you will sink or swim!"

Robin Hood spoke no word, for his nose and mouth were full of water, and he had no breath to spare. He swam to a bush of broom that overhung

the bank and dragged himself ashore. Meanwhile, the Friar leisurely waded out, shaking with mirth. Robin, angry, met him with bow bent and arrow aimed.

"Now, you false Friar, you shall die," he cried, grimly.

But the other never blenched. Raising up his buckler he said:

"Shoot on, you fine fellow. I tell you, if you shoot here all summer's day, I will never flee."

At that Robin lowered his bow. "No," said he, "on second thoughts, I will not shoot you dead where you stand, rascally hedge priest though you are. But with my good broadsword I will let your blood. Therefore, arm yourself and make ready."

"Not so hasty," said the Friar, calmly. "I'm ready and willing as a maid is to wed." He slowly set his steel cap upon his head, and then, grasping his

broadsword firmly in his great fist, he faced Robin with a bold front, bawling out: "Now, my crowing cockerel, I'll clip your comb and spurs, shake your wet feathers!"

Thereupon they rushed together with a loud clash of steel and flying sparks, but before long Robin saw that he must curb his hot blood or soon have it spilled; for the Friar, though angry, was calm and determined, bearing down Robin's guard with his heavy arm. So they fought from right to left, up and down, back and forth in the glade, with a savage fury and noise as if it were a whole company fighting.

Hour after hour the battle went on, with short pauses for rest, both panting and sweating, **eyeing** each other in silence, for neither had breath to waste in speech. From ten o'clock that morn had they struggled, and now past noon they were still tearing, slashing, and cutting with aching arms and tired backs; yet neither had a scratch.

19

"Hold!" bellowed the Friar. "Let us give up for a space, take a midday bite and quench our thirst. Then, to it again."

"Not so, you tough mountain of flesh," shouted bold Robin Hood. "Not till my sword has taken toll on some part of your fat body will I give over."

"Now hold your hand for a moment, my doughty fellow," said the Friar. "Will you not let me take off this hot steel cap to cool my brow? For the sweat is blinding me."

"Yes, do so, quickly," said Robin, the better pleased that now the broad shining poll would be a fair mark for his sword. Then the battle began afresh. Do all he could, Robin failed to strike the Friar's crown; and he in turn missed Robin a hundred times—and so the grim fight raged till four in the afternoon.

The ferns and woodland flowers were trodden into a shapeless mass among the soft, black loam. The song-birds had long flown away affrighted at the clashing din. At last bold Robin cried:

"Enough, enough, you curtal Friar! Give me leave

to set my horn to my mouth, and to blow three blasts upon it."

"That will I," said the curtal Friar, lowering the point of his sword. "I care not for your blast, though you blow till your eyes fall out."

So Robin set his horn to his lips and blew three loud blasts. Scarce had the Friar heard the echo when he saw two tall archers with shafts ready nocked come running over the grass.

"Whose men are these," cried he, "that come so hastily at your call?"

"These men are mine," said Robin Hood. "And what is that to thee?"

Then the curtal Friar saw that he had been tricked, but he was unabashed.

"A boon, a boon," he cried, mimicking Robin, with a shrewd glint in his eye, "like to that I granted you! Give me but leave to set my fist to my mouth and whistle thrice."

"That will I," said Robin, "for it is but just and fair."

So the Friar put his fist to his mouth and gave three loud whistles. The next moment there came half a dozen great mongrel dogs tearing along, barking loud as they drew nigh.

"Here, you cowardly villain," said the Friar, "are a couple of shaggy hounds for each of your men, and I myself will be enough for you. At 'em, my pets, tear their green jerkins to shreds, my hearties."

Thereupon, two great, ugly mastiffs climbed in front and back of Robin in a trice before he had time to defend himself or flee. At last, torn and ragged, he got him to a tree and sat, with legs astride a stout limb, watching Little John shoot at the fierce brutes. Then he saw what made him doubt his eyes, for the dogs leaped aside from the flying arrows, caught them in their mouths, and broke them in two.

"This is witchcraft," thought Robin, "and the Friar is a wizard, for never might dogs do so of their own nature." His wonder grew when he saw Will Scarlet step forth boldly toward the hounds with no weapon in his hand.

"Down, Beauty; down, Bess," cried Will, cuffing them right and left. Straightway the dogs began to cower down and fawn upon him, and gambolled about him as he stepped toward their master.

"What meaneth this?" said the Friar. "Have my dogs gone daft to love the company of thieves and cutthroats? Have I not, with their aid, kept Rubygill Abbey seven long year and more from baron, knight, and squire, and must I now yield myself to three beggarly yeoman that dare to beard me in my own dale? Tear them, tear their limbs asunder, good dogs!"

Will Scarlet now came forward, petting a great ugly hound.

"Come stout Friar," said he, "cease this brawling and curb your wagging tongue."

"What!" said the Friar. "Do my eyes behold young Will Gamwal in company with such a brace of deer-stealers? Now, I swear by holy Saint Boniface I will——"

"Peace, Friar, and listen," cried Will.

Then, pointing to Robin, he said: "This stout yeoman, who seems ill at ease perched in yonder tree, is none other than Robin Hood. The other tall fellow is Little John, his good righthand man; and they have come to bid you join our merry band of outlaws in Sherwood Forest. Call off your dogs and let us speak together and set matters right."

"Right Will," said the Friar, "I do know Robin Hood by report, but does he think to get me by cracking my bones? In truth I ache and am very sore."

At length, somewhat appeased and soothed by Will's manner and words, he whistled off his hounds. Then Robin climbed down the tree and, Little John with him, approached the Friar.

"For a holy man," said Robin, "truly you are the stoutest fighter that I ever clapped eyes upon."

"Nay, good Robin, you are the better man, for never was I so weary of any man in fight." With that he pushed forth his brawny palm, saying, "Right glad am I to meet the bold outlaws of Sherwood Forest."

"And now," said Robin, "all being well, we will go together in search of Friar Tuck, whom we came seeking; and you, holy Friar, must guide us."

"By my troth," laughed Will, "you have not far to seek, for that same holy friar now stands before you."

"What?" exclaimed Robin. "Surely you are not Friar Tuck!"

"The same," said the Friar, with a twinkle in his eye, "that gave you a duck in yon stream."

"And the same," laughed Robin, "that drained the bottle of good Rhenish wine. Truly my mouth waters to think on it."

"Then let us share another bottle" beamed the Friar, "before we take the road to Sherwood."

Robin Hood and the Knight

One day Robin, having gone forth with some of his merry men to see what rich men he could surprise and strip of their riches, saw a knight—Sir Richard of the Lees—coming towards him, heavy with grief.

"Good Sir Knight," said Robin, "why are you so sad?"

"Alas," said the knight, "my son had the misfortune to slay a man, and for his defence I had to borrow four hundred pounds from the abbot of St Mary's, York. Unless the money is paid on the morrow, my land will be taken, and I shall be a beggar and my wife with me."

"And what is your land worth, Sir Knight?"

"It is worth four hundred pounds a year."

"I' faith, the abbot wants a good deal for his loan!" cried Robin. Then––for it never took him long to make up his mind––he called Little John and commanded him to give the knight four hundred pounds, with some new clothes and a fine horse, and to go along to York as the knight's servant.

How Sir Richard's Estate Was Saved

"We will give my lord abbot an unpleasant surprise," said Robin. "He wants not your four hundred pounds, but your whole estate—the vile robber!"

So the knight, overwhelmed with joy and gratitude, promised to repay the money at the end of the year, and at once set out for York with Little John, to pay the abbot his debt.

Meanwhile, at the abbey of St Mary, the abbot and his cellarer were rubbing their hands in glee at the thought that the knight would not be able to pay. How vastly would the unlucky man's estate swell the riches of St Mary's!

Just as the cellarer was adding up to see what sum the land would be worth, the news came that the knight, Sir Richard of the Lees, was at the gate.

Sir Richard came into the abbot's presence humbly enough and pleaded for time to pay; for he wanted to see what would happen. Of course, the abbot and his cellarer refused to hear him, so eager were they to obtain possession of the land.

Then it was that Sir Richard brought out the bag of gold. The abbot and the cellarer looked at it, scarcely able to believe their eyes. The cellarer was so furious that he tried to set up some legal quibble to keep the knight from paying his debt after all, but there the money was, for all to see—and really the abbot and the cellarer could do nothing but take it.

Sir Richard met his wife, who was waiting at the

abbey gate, and together they went home, laughing merrily at the abbot's rage.

Some time afterwards the knight, having lived most carefully that he might save up the money, rode into the depths of Sherwood Forest to pay his debt to Robin Hood. Besides the four hundred pounds, he carried a present of one hundred bows and one hundred sheaves of arrows, each an ell long, with burnished heads, fledged with peacock's feathers, and notched with silver. With Sir Richard rode a hundred men, wearing his livery of white and red.

Now that very day Robin Hood, with two of his men, had gone to the high road to look for plunder. They saw two black-robed monks coming, each on a fine saddle-horse. These monks were on their way to London, carrying treasure packed, as was the custom, in hampers or casks on horses. They were attended by a guard of fifty-two archers.

But the fifty-two archers had no sooner set eyes on Robin and his men than they took to their heels and fled, leaving the treasure to be guarded only by the two monks, a little page boy, and a groom.

Robin laughed to himself—for St Mary's abbot had indeed sent him pay! At a blast of his horn, his companions gathered about him. Then he noticed that one of the monks was the cellarer who, according to Little John's report, had behaved so roughly to the unfortunate knight. But Robin was always polite.

"And pray, sirs, what money do you carry?" he asked the cellarer civilly.

"But twenty poor marks," said he, falsely.

"If you bear but twenty marks," Robin told him, "then I will double the sum; for to the poor, Robin Hood is always bountiful."

But he had no mind to take the monk's word for it. And when he came to look, behold, the treasure was worth some eight hundred pounds! Furthermore, he discovered that the monks were on the way to London to set the law in motion against Sir Richard of the Lees.

That settled the matter for Robin. He took the monks deep into the forest. There he entertained them royally—and sent them off stripped of every penny of their treasure! They turned mournfully back to the abbey, thinking that they could have dined as well— and more cheaply—at Doncaster.

Robin and his merry men were still laughing over this adventure when who should appear but Sir Richard himself, eager to pay his debt, and to present his fine gift of bows and arrows.

"I take not a penny," cried Robin boisterously. "The good cellarer of St Mary's has already paid me! As for the bows and arrows, I accept them gladly, and for them you shall have another four hundred pounds."

Allan-a-Dale and His Bride

One day on the highway Little John overtook a young gentleman and asked him what moneys he had.

"I have but five shillings and a ring," said the youth.

"If that be true," said Little John, "then I want nothing from you."

Just then Robin came up and asked the young man why he looked so sad.

"Ah, you may well ask!" cried young Allan-a-Dale. "This ought to be my wedding morning; but my bride is being given away by her father to an old knight who can offer gold by the bushel for her."

"And where is the church," asked Robin, "in which this wedding is to take place?"

"It is but five miles from here," said Allan, and the tears streamed from his eyes.

Robin Hood would have no tears, but he told young Allan to keep with his merry men and follow him, when summoned, to the church. Then Robin disguised himself cunningly as a harpist, and went off to the home of the bride's father to ask whether he might play music at the wedding feast.

"By all means," said the father. "Here is the bishop; he can tell whether you are a good harpist or no."

"Nay," cried Robin, "there shall be no music from this harp of mine until I have set eyes on the bride and the bridegroom."

The bride came in, pale as snow and drooping with sadness. The bridegroom, who escorted her, was old and wizened as a winter-tossed oak.

"Now, now!" cried Robin, "this is no fit match, sir! Would you wed a snowdrop with an old thistle? By my faith, this bride shall choose her own bridegroom."

At that he blew a lusty blast on his horn, and twenty-four archers answered the call. They were led by Little John, and among them was Allan-a-Dale.

"Now, sweet bride," said Robin, "will you have yonder gnarled trunk for your dear, or will you choose this youth, with five hundred pounds in his pouch and brave young limbs to work for you?"

"Allan! It is Allan!" cried the bride. "He is my love and my dear!"

Allan-a-Dale knelt at her feet and took her hand. The aged bridegroom glanced at the terrified father, then at the sturdy archers, then at Robin Hood— who was merry-eyed enough but resolute in every muscle. Then the bridegroom begged leave to be let off from his bargain.

"But indeed," cried the bride's father, "she cannot marry any but you, sir, for no bishop can wed a pair unless they have been asked three times in church."

"That is soon done!" cried Little John. Then he led the way to the church, and, standing under the desk, he published the banns seven times instead of three, just to make sure.

Then the bishop married the bride and Allan-a-Dale, and every one of the merry men was bidden to the wedding feast.

The Fair Maid Marian

Now Robin Hood loved a certain maiden dearly, and her name was Maid Marian. Maid Marian loved Robin too, but her father would not let her marry him. Bold Robin had given her a ring, and she had sworn to marry no man until King Richard should be freed from his prison and come home again.

One day, as Robin strode on adventure through the wood, disguised as a husbandman, a proud youth appeared in the forest glade, and Robin challenged him. The youth answered him hotly, and drew sword. As the singer of the old ballad tells us:

They drew out their swords, and to cutting they
    went,
    At least an hour or more,
That the blood ran apace from bold Robin's face,
    And the youth was wounded sore.

"Hold!" cried Robin at last—for indeed he was sorry to hurt so brave a lad—"Hold, fair youth! Let us fight no more."

"Why," faltered the brave lad, ready to faint from his labour, "who are you, then?"

"My name is Robin Hood," the outlaw answered with a laugh, "Now you know—"

But the stranger gave a cry and stretched out one white hand; and on a finger of it Robin saw the ring he had given to Maid Marian!

"That ring—"

"You gave me, Robin!"

Then it was that Maid Marian fell forward, and Robin clasped her in his arms.

"Maid Marian—you have come to me—into the wild forest?" he cried in joy and wonder. "And how have I greeted you!"

"Yes, I have come," she said.

Robin blew his horn, and up dashed his merry men.

"Allan-a-Dale," he cried, "I helped you win your wife. Let your wife now look after my bride. She shall wed me—"

"Never!" It was the high-spirited girl herself who interrupted him. "Never—until the King himself shall come to give me away! Would you have me forget my vow?"

"Be it so," said Robin then, and kissed her tenderly. "Yet to-night, when Maid Marian has rested from her brave fight with a quarrelsome husbandman, we shall crown her queen of the forest."

But when she returned home her father, the Baron of Arlingford, was furious. Marian was confined to the castle. He had no intention of letting his daughter marry an outlaw. Her love of the forest and the chase, which he had never before dis-couraged, was now a matter of serious alarm to him, for he loved his daughter the bewitching Marian very much.

"If you coop me up here, I shall die like a lonely swan on a pool," she cried.

In other words Marian had no intention of giving up her wild sweetheart even though she was prepared to wait to be married.

"I must go to the woods, father," she insisted.

"Must!" said the Baron, "I say you must not!"

"But I am going," said Marian.

"I will have the drawbridge up," said the Baron.

"Then I will swim the moat," said Marian.

"But I will seal the gates," said the Baron.

"Then I shall leap from the battlements," said she.

"So, I will lock you in an upper chamber," said the Baron.

"And I will shred the tapestry, and let myself down."

"Right, I shall lock you in a turret," said the Baron, "where you shall only see light through a loophole."

"Ah, but through the loophole I shall take flight, like a young eagle from its eyrie. Understand, father, let me go freely and I will return willingly, but if you force me to slip through a loophole, you will never see me again."

Marian had her own way. She ranged at liberty, but always kept her promise to return home. This had the effect of giving her father great confidence in her—but it was about to end abruptly.

The Baron was one morning munching his way through breakfast, when his ears were assailed by a tremendous clamour. A large party of armed men on the other side of the moat were calling in the king's name that the drawbridge be lowered.

The Baron walked along the battlements until he faced his visitors across the moat. As soon as they saw him they yelled again. "Lower the drawbridge and raise the portcullis at once."

"For what and for whom," asked the Baron.

"The Sheriff of Nottingham," said the leader, "lies in bed grievously bruised, many of his men are wounded and some slain. We are here to apprehend William Gamwal, Father Michael and your daughter, Marian Fitzwater, accomplices in this breach of the king's peace."

"Rubbish!" roared the Baron. "What do you mean by coming here with your cock and bull stories —my daughter bruising the Sheriff of Nottingham indeed. You are a set of rascals, be off with you, leave at once!"

"Lord Fitzwater," cried one, "take heed how you resist lawful authority. We shall yet prove ourselves."

By this time the Baron's men had flocked to the battlements, with long-bows, cross-bows, slings and stones, and Marian with her bow and quiver at their head. The assailants, observing the castle so well defended, deemed it expedient to get out. They turned their horses about and galloped away. The Baron turned to his daughter,

"Explain this, Marian, my dear, for I fear there is trouble here."

Marian told him William Gamwal and she had been in the forest, joining in a merry May dance with Friar Michael and a group of foresters, when

the Sheriff of Nottingham burst on the scene with a retinue of fifty men and tried to arrest one of the party. All immediately resisted, Marian herself wounding one of the knights.

"I see," said the Baron, "and I can guess who that forester was—this bold Robin, this courteous Robin, this thief of Sherwood Forest was behind it all. You'll hunt no more in that company, my girl. No more games and feasts, these pranks could mean the loss of my castle and lands, so an end to it I say!"

But Lord Fitzwater was soon to become an outlaw himself. A week later, the heralding of trumpets and waving of banners brought an eminent visitor to the castle gate. Prince John, brother of Richard the Lion Heart, King of England, was announced. Marian's spirits dropped, for on a previous visit to the castle, John had made it very apparent that he wished her to return with him to London. Both she and her father resisted his design, for they were constant to Richard, who was absent on another crusade.

35

That evening there were bitter words. The Baron insisted that his daughter remain where she was; the Prince, almost shrieking in his frustration, suddenly struck the father down and had him banished to a turret prison and a guard placed over him. The Baron's own men could do nothing to help, since it would put their master's life in jeopardy if they attempted to fight, but young William Gamwal, friend of Marian, heard the voices raised. He knew of John's infatuation for Marian, and, feeling that Robin Hood should be informed about the visit of the Prince, left the castle, ostensibly to return to Gamwal Hall, but in fact to seek out the Outlaw of Sherwood. He located Robin Hood just as darkness closed over the trees.

"Did any of Prince John's men see you leave?" said Robin at length.

"I think not," said William, "in fact no one would have known I was there."

"Then return, go in the open, say you are visiting Marian. Then, with darkness, put some ropes over the battlements. You'll have friends there who'll help. Little John and several of my men will swim the moat and you can draw us up to the top of the wall. Now, sleep, for there is much to be arranged tomorrow."

There was no reason to suspect Will Gamwal of being anything but harmless, so he was admitted into the castle with the excuse of having a message for the Lady Marian, and that night, several ropes were suspended from the battlements, and loyal supporters of the Baron stood by to hand up the brave fellows who would attempt the rescue of Lord Fitzwater and his daughter.

Prince John was not accompanied by many soldiers. His advantage lay in holding the Baron prisoner. So few patrolled the castle walls. Most drank or slept while the Prince attempted to persuade the lovely Marian to follow the direction of his own wishes.

"What do you intend to do with my father?" asked Marian, "you cannot keep him prisoner in his own castle."

"I do not intend to, sweet lady. Tomorrow he goes with me to London, and there he stays until you follow. I will keep him for eternity if necessary."

Marian gave no sign that she had noticed the door latch being raised, and when the heavy door began to inch open, her composure was admirable to behold, and until a dagger was placed at the throat

of the Prince, she made barely a movement. Then she was all vigour and activity.

"Robin! William said you would come—I've waited."

"Little John has your father safe. Will is enlisting the aid of the Baron's men. In a moment there will be a battle and we'll pitch this cur and his rabble into the moat," said Robin.

All transpired as Robin had planned, and from the castle walls they watched the soaked and wretched Prince stagger along the road with his defeated followers.

"Prince John will brand me as an outlaw for this night's work," remarked the Baron as Robin and his men were preparing to depart.

"Then join our company whenever you wish, my Lord," laughed the outlaw, "for you will never find a more loyal band of rascals."

The Baron looked glum, but he knew that with Prince John and the Sheriff of Nottingham ranged against him, these staunch rogues might be his only allies. He took the outlaw's hand.

Robin Hood and the Beggar

Now it fell upon a fair afternoon that Robin went alone through a fern-clad forest path. After a while he got upon the high-road, where he met a beggar going sturdily along at a good pace, looking neither to the right nor to the left, noticing no one as he strode on his way. In his hand he held a pike-staff that was both stout and strong, while wound about his body was a clouted cloth folded many times, making an excellent covering from wind and rain. Tied to a leathern strap there hung from his neck a large mealbag, firmly fastened to a stout, broad buckle, and upon his head were three hats stuck fast together, one above the other, so that wherever he went little did he care either for sun or for rain.

When good Robin spied this oddly attired stranger he stepped boldly right in front of him, for he had a shrewd thought that the beggar was not so poor as he seemed.

"Stay," said Robin, "stay awhile and speak with me."

But the beggar, making as if he had not heard him, went but the faster on his way, without so much as a turn of his head.

"Well," said Robin, "you show me scant courtesy. You must stop, for I have something to say to you."

"By my three hats," cried the beggar, in a harsh voice, "to stay I have no will, for it is getting late, and it is far to my lodging house. Should they have supper before I get there, I shall get no food."

"Now," said good Robin, "I see well that in thinking only of your own supper, you have no care of mine. All this day have I eaten no food, and I have nowhere to lie this night. To the tavern would I go but I have no money. Sir stranger, you must lend me some till we meet again."

The beggar answered peevishly: "I have no money to lend; I think you are as young as I and as strong, I warrant. If you fast till I lend you money, you shall eat naught this year."

"Then," said bold Robin, "since we are together here, if you have but one farthing I'll take it from you ere you go. Come, beggar, cease to stand there staring me in the face; or I will open up all the bags, your tag-rags and bobtails, and rip them to pieces with my hands. Should you make an outcry, I vow by the saints to try how far a broad arrow can pierce a beggar's skin."

The beggar looked at Robin with a wry smile upon his face and made answer:

"Far better let me be; for do not think I care a straw, or be afraid for your nip-crooked tree that you call a bow, nor that I care any whit for your sticks that you call arrows. Here do I defy you to do me harm—for all your loud talk you will get nothing from me but ill."

Such fearless words from a ragged beggar roused Robin's wrath. Straightway he nocked a broad arrow and bent his great bow. But e'er it was drawn a span, the beggar with his stout pike-staff reached forward with so swift a stroke that the bow burst in two. Nothing daunted, Robin with a bound darted to strike down the beggar with his sword, but that proved likewise vain, for the fellow with his pike-staff struck such a fierce blow on Robin's hand that his sword fell to the ground.

Robin could not speak a word, for he was sick at heart and faint from bitter pain. Yet still the beggar with his terrible pike-staff laid lusty blows upon his side and back, till at last Robin fell down on the soft sward, lying helpless and bleeding at the mercy of his terrible foe.

"Stand up, stand up," the beggar man said; "'tis a shame to go to rest. In truth, I think it were best to stay till you get your money. Then go to the tavern and buy both food and wine with the beggar's money. There you can boast of what you did get in the forest."

Robin answered ne'er a word, but lay still as a stone. Closed were both his eyes, and his cheeks were pale as any clay. With a few more blows upon his body the beggar thought him dead, and leaving him to lie stark and still, his face upturned to the sky, he strode on his way.

Now it so happened that by good chance three of Robin's band came walking by the way and found their master lying on the ground, wounded, bleeding, and senseless.

"Who has done this foul deed, comrades?" said one. "Let us take our dear master up, and carry him

to yon brook, that we may sprinkle water on his face and so bring him to life.'' So they took up good Robin, who made a piteous moan, while blood gushed forth from his mouth and nose. Yet though they searched all over his body, they found no cuts, but many cruel bruises. When his brow had been bathed with cold water, Robin at last came to his senses enough to speak a little.

''Tell us, dear master,'' said his men, ''tell us what is the matter, and how you fell into such an evil situation.''

Robin sighed deep e'er he began to tell of his disgrace.

''For twenty years and more have I been outlaw and forester in this wood, yet I was never so hard beaten as you have found me here. A beggar with a clouted cloak hath with his pike-staff so mauled my back that I fear 'twill never be well. He went o'er yon hill, and upon his head, he carried three hats. If ever you loved your master, go now to revenge me of this vile deed and bring him back to me again. Take care that he does not escape.''

"One of us shall stay with you, because you are in no state to be left alone, and the other two, I warrant, shall bring the villain beggar back to use as you will."

"Now, by my faith," said good Robin, "enough has been said. Take good heed, for I fear you will both be evil paid if he gets a chance to swing his wicked tree around your noddles."

"Be not afraid, dear master, that we two can be bested by any base beggar that carries naught but a staff! You shall shortly see that his staff will stand him in no stead. He shall be brought back again, fast bound, to see if you will have us slay him."

"Be sly then," said Robin, "and by stealth work your way into his path before he is aware."

The two outlaws then left Robin, clinging to a tree

like a poor, tottering old man. Now the beggar had mended his pace and was striding along over the hill, giving no thought to the trouble he had caused and only anxious to reach his lodging ere nightfall. The two outlaws ran at full speed by a lower path, careless of the mud and briars along the way, going a distance of over three miles. Then, turning to a

little clump of bushes in a glen that the beggar must surely pass, they hid themselves close behind trees on each side of the path, standing ready till the beggar drew nigh. After a little they saw him coming, and just as he got betwixt them both leaped upon him.

Taken off his guard, the beggar was so afraid that he dared not move. He could not run, he could not

wield his staff. He was not sure but other outlaws might be near; so in despair, thinking that at last his life's end was near at hand, he began to crave mercy.

"Grant me my life," he pleaded, "and hold away that ugly knife. I never harmed you in all my life, neither by night nor day, and indeed you do a great sin if you slay a poor silly beggar."

"You lie, false and cruel varlet," cried the outlaw who held his staff. "You have near slain the gentlest and kindest man that e'er was born. Back again to him you shall be led, fast bound with thongs, to see if he will have you slain or bid us hang you."

Then the beggar thought that all was done with him, though if he could but escape out of their hands and get hold of his staff he was sure that he would teach them another game. While they made ready to bind him he cudgelled his brains for some wily scheme to free himself. The only way that came into his mind was to tempt them with some money; so he said:

"Brave gentlemen, be good to me, and let me go. It helps you not a flea to take a beggar's blood. 'Twas but to save mine own hide that I did hurt your master, and listen, good friends—I will give you a recompense that shall make you rich if you will but set me free and do me no more harm. I will give you a hundred pounds, and much more odd silver that I have gathered these many years. Under this clouted cloak I have it, far hidden beneath its folds next to my skin and also in the bottom of my meal-bag."

To this neither of the young men answered a word, but each looked at his companion to see whether he would be false to his honour and disgrace the band. One argued, "We will take the money to our captain and tell him that the beggar is slain." The other said: "Our orders were 'Bring him back alive or dead'."

At last they agreed to yield to the beggar's counsel and let him go, then follow after and take him again by stealth when they had his money; for, being swift of foot, they might easily overtake him.

"False knave," said one, "say no more, but get the money and count it out. 'Tis little enough to pay for the ill turn you have done our master; yet come what may, if you give us the money now we will not take you back."

So the beggar thanked them right heartily, and straightway set about loosening his clouted cloak to spread it on the ground. Then he took from his neck a bag containing over two pecks of meal, which he set down upon the cloak. Opening wide the bag, he bent down and felt in every nook and corner for the money. Both young men drew their faces closer to see the gold appear, when of a sudden the beggar lifted out two great handfuls of meal and flung it in their faces, blinding them so that they could do naught with their hands save strive to wipe the meal from eyes, nose, and mouth. In a trice the beggar grasped his pike-staff and, with a gleeful laugh, cried:

"Now, my pretty pair of blades, if I've done you wrong in mealing your clothes, with my staff I will strike off the meal again."

With that, he began to ply his staff, filling the air with meal from their bodies as his mighty blows fell on their shoulders, necks, and arms. The young outlaws, half blinded and choked, could do nought to help themselves. They turned and ran with all the speed they could muster, leaving the beggar shaking his staff in the air and calling upon them to stay awhile and get well dusted.

"What's all this haste?" he cried. "Stay a while, I'll pay you with a right good will until you have had enough and to spare. The shakings of my meal-bag have by chance blown into your eyes, but what of that? I have a good pike-staff that will soon make them clear."

Thus he went on entreating them in right loving fashion to tarry, but the young outlaws heard him not, for they were far away. Since the night was creeping on apace, it would be vain to follow and attack him now, so they thought it wise to return, and with sad hearts and downcast looks they got them back to their master.

"Well, my comrades," asked Robin, "how did you speed in your quest?"

They answered him, "Full ill, and we were evil paid."

"That cannot be," said Robin. "A man would think to look at your clothes that you have been working for the miller. Tell me the matter truly— how did you fare, and what have you done with the bold beggar I sent you for."

The young men drooped down, hanging their heads for very shame, and could not speak a word. Then, with true anger in his voice, Robin said:

"Because I fell beneath the cudgel of this beggar fiend I think you feared he would serve you in the same fashion."

At these words, so true and so just, the young men

confessed, and told Robin the truth all to the end—
how the beggar blinded them with the meal, how he
basted their bones so sore to dust it from their
clothes, and how they fled to the forest.

Robin cried out: "For shame! We are dishonoured
forever. Help me to lift my weary bones, and take me
quickly to my bower."

As they carried him along the path he thought he
would have revenge, yet even in his pain he smiled to
think that two of his merry young men had got a
taste of that beggar's pike-staff besides himself.

Robin Sells Pots and Dishes

Robin was angered to the depths of his heart at thought of the beggar's brutishness, for he himself had never in his life struck a fallen foe, to say nothing of beating a man who lay senseless and helpless at his feet. Yet he thought: "I was to blame! I brought it upon my own head, and must perforce bear the pain I got." Such were his thoughts as he painfully dragged his aching bones along, with the help of his two followers, back through the forest to the oak glade. It seemed an age before he got there,

and twice he fainted from weakness. Little John met them with a very sad face, and he wept to see his master in such a plight. Then with his strong arms he fairly carried Robin to his bower, there to lie a month or more till his swollen, bruised body grew strong and well once more.

Many a time he bemoaned himself bitterly to Little John because he could not go abroad. Then, with comforting words, mixed with a spice of sound advice, Little John would soothe him, saying:

"In truth, my dear master, you are too prone to fight with quarterstaff against a foe more used to that weapon. With a good long bow, the case is different, for you would always be the victor."

"I cannot in cold blood," said Robin, "send a shaft through a foe's body with but a pace or two between us. Once I slew a man, and never again will I take life save as dire need or in the heat of combat. But, by heaven, I will no longer lie here like a cat tied in a bag."

Again Little John would gently chide his master, bidding him wait at least till he could stand upon his legs without wobbling. "For," said he, "our treasure is ample, our wants are all supplied, and the men content. Be patient, therefore, for in a week or more, once again you will be strong—long before the wintry wind blows through the glade."

At last, toward the end of summer, the three best doctors of the band—Friar Tuck, Arthur-a-Bland, and Little John—agreed that Robin was well enough to go upon short trips to hunt the deer. Shooting contests were held and games resumed, as a change from the more serious work of gathering in the winter stores. It was now the middle of August. The days were warm, the evenings long and light till ten o'clock, so that the band was in a merry mood, as was their wont when all went well.

Thus it was that, on the next day, a bright, fair morn being a Saturday and a market-day, Robin, Little John, and others of the band set forth toward the great highway that ran along the forest edge, to gather tolls from any that were able to pay, and give away, for charity's sake, to those in dire need. Presently they saw a man sitting on the shafts of a rude little cart pulled by a pony. The cart was filled with mugs, basins, and other pottery vessels, which the man bought very cheap at Stoke, where they were made, and carted from town to town to sell at a good profit. He was singing a merry ditty, now and then whipping up his pony that he might reach

Nottingham market in good time. It was plain by his looks that he could take good care of his pots as well as himself.

"Here comes a stout potter," said Robin, "he has crossed this forest many a time, yet has never paid one penny of passage money to us. He shall not escape us this time, I warrant."

"Better let him pass, good master," said Little John. "I met the fellow once at Wentbridge, and he gave me three such clouts that I want no more from him, though I gave him clout for clout. I will lay forty shillings there is not a man among us that can make the potter pay toll."

Bold Robin could not let that pass. "Here are forty shillings," he cried, "and more will I lay that I can make that bold potter pay some token for his passage."

"He will give you his staff for a token! I vow that from him you will get no other pay, my master," said John. But Robin, without more words, strode to the middle of the high road, and, standing firm as a rock till the potter drew nigh, laid his hand on the bridle, bidding the man stand.

"Fellow," bawled the potter, "what do you want?"

"All these three years and more, potter," said Robin, "you have passed by this way, yet never paid a penny toll to us."

"What is your name?" said the potter, "and what is your right to ask for passage money on the King's highway?"

"Robin Hood is my name, and king of these woods, to whom it is your duty to pay toll."

"Not a bad farthing shall you get from me," said

the potter, "let go my horse, or I vow to strike it off with my staff."

Straightway leaping down from the shaft, he unstrapped from under the cart a stout pike-staff, saying in angry tones:

"Now, bold outlaw, take your hand from my horse."

Robin drew his sword and, with a buckler upon his arm, advanced to meet the potter, who with a powerful balk-stroke smote off the shield. In a trice the haughty pike-staff was brought down with another fierce blow on Robin's neck as he stooped to get his buckler again. So stiff was the stroke that it sent Robin sprawling on the ground.

"Let us go to help our master," cried Little John, "or yon potter will do him harm."

Then, running toward Robin, with shouts of laughter, he said: "Who has won the wager now? Shall I have the forty shillings, or shall you have mine?"

"Yes, were they a hundred shillings," said Robin, "They are all yours."

"There is little courtesy," said the potter, "as I have heard wise men say, to take from a poor yeoman what little he has while driving along the highway."

"By my faith, you speak the truth," said Robin, "and from this day forth you shall never be hindered; for a friendship would I have with you, and good payment will I give. Make exchange with me of your clothing, for I will sell pots in Nottingham town, and you shall stay here in the forest to feast on good venison. When I come back, if I sell all, you shall be the gainer."

"To that I will agree," said the potter. "You shall find me an honest fellow; and if you can sell my pots well, come back again when you have done so."

Then spoke Little John and his comrades, "Master, take care and beware of the Sheriff, for he would gladly slay you by fair means or foul. Alone, you will be in great jeopardy."

"Nay, my good comrades," said Robin, "let me be, for by the help of our Good Lady, to Nottingham I will go."

So Robin changed clothes with the potter, and, with some touches here and there to make a better disguise, he jumped on the shaft of the cart and drove away in a jolly good mood, singing a merry song. When he reached Nottingham, he drew up his horse close by the Sheriff's gate, and gave it some

oats and hay. Then setting forth his pots, both large and small, upon the cart, so as to make the best show, he began to cry out:

"Crocks and pots, jugs and mugs, who wants to buy? I give one extra, no matter how large or small."

This way the bargaining was new to the wives and widows of Nottingham, and soon drew a large crowd round his cart. Not content with throwing in an extra pot, Robin sold pots worth five pence for three pence. This made the women gape, both old and

young; and while they bought they said to each other slyly, "This potter will never thrive at this rate."

"You will have none left ere long, if you sell so cheap," said one buxom wife.

"For that cause came I hither," said smiling Robin, "to sell all I have." And he did sell so fast that before noon only five pieces were left.

"Well done, you cunning potter," said Robin to himself.

"These five unsold pots will I give with my compliments to the Sheriff's wife." And so, in fact he did.

"Sir," said the Sheriff's wife, with a tender smile on good Robin. "When you come to this town again I shall buy what pots I want from you, so much do I like your courtesy. Your kindness is truly great, and I would like you to come and dine with the Sheriff and me."

"God's mercy, good lady," said Robin, "your bidding shall be done."

Then a young maid carried in the pots, and Robin followed the Sheriff's wife to the hall, where he met the Sheriff, who spoke to him heartily:

"Look," said the lady, "what this potter has given us for a present—five pots, both large and small."

"He is full welcome," said the Sheriff. "Let us enter and go to dine."

As they sat at the table, with merry talk and laughter, two of the Sheriff's men began to speak of a prize of forty shillings offered for the best shooting

with the long-bow among the townspeople that day. "Now, as I am a true Christian man," Robin said to himself, "this shooting-match will I see."

When they had appeased their hunger upon the very best of bread, ale, and wine, to the shooting-butts they all went to see who would win the prize. The Sheriff's men began to shoot, but they were very poor archers, and none of them got nearer the mark than half the length of a long-bow. The potter looked on with great contempt; and when the Sheriff said, "What think you, good potter, of our archery?" he made answer:

"In plain truth, it seems to me to be very poor. If I had a bow, with one shot I would beat them all."

"I warrant you shall have a bow for that one shot," said the Sheriff, "the best you may choose from such as we have. You seem strong and stalwart as any here." He then bade a yeoman that stood by bring some bows for the potter to choose from.

"'Tis the best here," said Robin, as he took up a bow, "though 'tis a poor, weak thing. Nevertheless, with it I will make good my word."

So without more ado he strode up to the line, side by side with the Sheriff's men, who smiled and twitted him upon his impudence in daring to shoot in such company. The potter answered naught, but, pulling the string to his ear, he carelessly shot the arrow within a foot of the mark. Then the Sheriff's men tried once more with little better success. When the potter again took his place to shoot, they had

greater respect for his skill and waited anxiously to see what he would do. Taking much more careful aim, he let fly the shaft and cleft the wand apart, much to the wonder of the Sheriff's men, who thought it great shame that a common potter should win the prize from them. But the Sheriff and his wife were both mightily pleased, and said:

"You are a man worthy to bear a bow anywhere."

"In my cart," he made answer, "I have a bow that I had from Robin Hood."

"Knowest you Robin Hood?" asked the surprised Sheriff. "Tell me of him."

"A hundred times," replied the potter, "have I shot with him under his trysting-tree."

"By my faith," said the Sheriff, "I would give a hundred pounds to have that villainous outlaw stand before me here."

"I would win that hundred pounds," said the potter, "and tomorrow after we have taken our breakfast, if you will go with me I will show you Robin Hood."

"I will pay you well," said the Sheriff, joyfully. "By my faith, you shall not repent of serving me in this matter."

Upon the morrow the potter was early ready with horse and cart. Taking leave of the Sheriff's wife, he thanked her heartily for her good cheer.

"Good dame," said he, "for my love to you, be pleased to wear this gold ring."

"Gracious, good sir, I yield to your wish, for I know the Sheriff's heart was never so light to see the fair forest as in the company of so gallant a companion."

So the Sheriff, on his horse, and the potter, seated in his little cart, both set off for Sherwood.

The morning was bright and warm, and the little birds sang merrily among the green leaves. "The greenwood is a merry place," said Robin, "for a man that has nought to spend, and by the sound of my horn we shall soon know if Robin Hood be near at hand." Then he set his horn to his mouth and blew a blast both loud and long, that could be heard far down the forest glade.

"I hear my master's call," said Little John. "Let us haste, and run to see if all be well." Presently through an opening of the trees they appeared before the potter and addressed him, saying:

"Master, how have you fared in Nottingham? Have you sold all the wares?"

"Yes, Little John. Look you and see. I have brought the Sheriff of Nottingham in exchange for my goods."

"He is welcome," said Little John. "Such tidings make us glad."

It was then that the Sheriff saw the trick that the potter had served him, and he thought he would rather have given a hundred pounds than to have met Robin Hood that day.

"Had I known," said he, "that you were Robin Hood, you would not have seen this fair forest for a thousand years."

"I know that well," said Robin, laughing. "Therefore you shall leave your horse and other gear with us. You came on horseback, and back you shall go afoot to give my greetings to your good wife at home. I shall give her a white palfrey, and you may tell her that had she used less courtesy you would have fared much more sadly at our hands." Thus the Sheriff parted from Robin, and to Nottingham he took his way.

His wife was there to give him a welcome. "How did you fare in the greenwood?" she said. "Have you brought Robin Hood home?"

The Sheriff swore a great oath and said: "I have been basely scorned, and tricked of all the moneys I took to the greenwood. My large, fine horse, its gold trappings, my pouch with a hundred pounds were all stripped from me amid the jeers and merry quips of that vile band."

Upon that, the good dame laughed loud and long.

"Now," said she, "he has then been well paid for all those pots he gave to us."

So we leave the unhappy Sheriff and return to the greenwood, where Robin called the potter to him, saying, "Good potter, what were the pots worth that I sold in Nottingham market?"

"They were worth two pounds, but I should have traded and made more by my traffic," said the potter.

"You shall have ten pounds," said Robin. "And remember bold potter, when you come to the greenwood you shall ever be welcome."

So they parted as the best of friends, each well satisfied with the other. Then the potter set off blithe and merry on his way back to Stoke, to get his cart refilled with pots and crocks, hoping to make as good a trade again. "But of that," thought he, "I have grave doubts—there is but one Robin Hood."

Robin and Sir Guy of Gisbourne

This latest clever trick of Robin Hood's was the straw that broke the Sheriff's patience. Each man that sat at meat with him or passed him upon the streets of Nottingham town seemed to be Robin Hood in disguise. The disgrace was so much the harder to bear because his wife found delight in constantly talking of the comely, courteous outlaw and his present of the gold ring, which she still wore. So the Sheriff longed for a dire revenge, and searched eagerly for some means whereby he might put an end at once and forever to the troubles he had borne for twenty-odd years.

At last he decided to give a great feast and invite as many as would come of the barons and knights of the shire. For he thought that if they would not help him with money and men they might at least advise him how best to rid the nearby forests of these pests. He had often tried to get the aid of bold yeoman of his town, but they had flatly said him nay, for many of them had received kindness from Robin and his men. So the Sheriff bade his servants prepare the banquet, to which came not a few of the barons and knights.

When they had eaten the good things and drunk well the wine, the Sheriff arose and addressed them, laying bare all his woe. At this one brave knight got upon his feet and said:

"Sir Sheriff, while we grieve with you in this trouble, not one of us can soil his knightly hands to draw sword in so mean a cause—to wit, the catching of a rascally deer-stealer. Such base deeds are meet for your yeoman or the King's foresters."

"Oft have I promised them much gold," said the Sheriff, "but they either will not, or dare not, encounter this band. Yea, they all turn pale at the name of Robin Hood."

"In faith," said the knight, "I know not any other means whereby you can have your will unless some knight down at the heels for want of friends and gold were willing to lead a company of trained men to the forest and drive the outlaws away."

"Do you, Sir Knight, know of such a one?"

"There is one," replied the knight, "who would do your bidding, if the prize were great. This Sir Guy of Gisbourne is bold enough to do any deed you may set for him, nor will he value his knightly honour above five hundred pounds."

After the guests had gone the Sheriff lost no time in seeking out this Sir Guy, and on the morrow he sent a messenger on horseback to the little market-town of Gisbourne in the West Riding of Yorkshire. Now Sir Guy was poor; he had wasted his substance in riotous living; but, instead of repenting, he was ever ready to do any deed, however base, not only because he needed gold, but for the mere love of doing evil.

In his native town he was feared by every man, and abhorred by every wife, widow, or lass. Besides his wickedness he was the ugliest creature in merry England. His naturally savage features were scarred by many wounds and cuts, for he had been to the wars in the Holy Land, in Ireland, in Scotland, and in the South. Everywhere he went, ever fighting; yet he seemed to bear a charmed life. Utterly cruel, with a black and stony heart, his bold and fierce demeanour affrighted all men. When he was angry, his face and scars turned a livid blue, so awful to look upon that his foes took him for a demon risen from the regions below. It was his wont to go clad from head to foot in the hide of a horse. The ears stood up from a hood, at the back of which hung the mane, and below was the horse's tail. This body covering was tanned soft with the hair outside, so that he who wore it looked more a beast than a man. Such, then, was the evil Sir Guy, whom the Sheriff's messenger went to seek as a leader to fight and destroy the good Robin Hood and his outlaws.

When he reached the little town of Gisbourne, the messenger had little trouble in learning the whereabouts of him he sought.

"What is the price?" roared Sir Guy, when he had heard the tale. "Repeat to me the sum, that I be not mistaken."

"Five hundred pounds in good coin," said the messenger, "for the living body of Robin Hood, or his head if you slay him."

"'Tis a fair sum for so slight a deed," said Sir Guy slowly, "and, to be brief, I will do the Sheriff's will. The outlaw's head is mine; the money is earned. Do you hear that?" Down came his fist with such a crack on the table that the messenger nearly jumped out of his skin.

"Yes, Sir Guy, I hear, and doubt it not."

"What, ho! knavish hind!" he shouted to a servant. "Get my horse, and furnish him for combat. Get me my two Irish daggers and my longest brown Egyptian blade. There is work afoot for us, so choose the toughest yew long-bow and double-pointed shafts, and be ready at once."

All was soon in readiness, and before long the two were riding back toward Nottingham, which they reached late on the following day. Meanwhile, the Sheriff had not been idle. He foresaw that Sir Guy would willingly do a work so much to his taste, especially for a prize so large. He had already gathered together a hundred of his own men and two hundred of the King's foresters. The latter he would place under the command of Sir Guy, and he himself would lead his own servants. He was no coward, though his men were not of the same metal.

When the knight presented himself, the Sheriff's joy was unbounded. "Such a fierce-looking monster did I ne'er behold," he thought. "Surely he will slay bold Robin." Then he said aloud:

"Thrice welcome are you, Sir Knight of Gisbourne. Let us dine and then talk of what we have to do."

So they went into the hall, where Sir Guy seated himself opposite the place where the Sheriff's wife would sit. Unsheathing his two Irish daggers, he laid one shining blade close beside his platter, the other beside his wine-goblet, and prepared to eat. The Sheriff's wife had been told of this man, and what he was about to do, but she was so afraid at the knives and the fellow's evil looks that she fainted dead away in the arms of her husband, who helped the servants to carry her away from the table.

"What is the matter with your good lady, Sir Sheriff?" asked Guy.

"I believe," said he, "she is overcome with joy to know that the outlaw's end is near."

"Ay, by the bones of Saint Withold!" growled Sir Guy, "of truth it is so. But tell me, what manner of man is this Robin Hood, famed as he is to far and wide? Is he big of bone and broad of chest, like King Richard, that all men fear him?"

"No, by the mass," said the Sheriff, "he is as mild as a sucking pig and gentle as a lamb. The cooing turtle-dove could not match him in soft persuasion.

But mark you well, Sir Knight, no fox was ever so sly; no adder creeping through the damp sward is so silent as his footfall on the grass."

"And what of his prowess?" asked Sir Guy. "I have heard of his skill in archery, but doubt it."

"Doubt it not, Sir Knight, for no archer lives, nor ever lived, that can match him. With the broadsword and buckler, and also with the quarterstaff, he has men in combat the strongest and best in merry England, and he has drawn them to his band. I know

not of any means to take him save to outnumber him. Outwit him—'tis impossible! Outfight him—'tis doubtful! If you can meet him alone, you may have the better of him. Indeed, rather would I see it done in such a manner than in any other. It were well that you should go before us to tempt the wily fox to single combat. It is well known that he loves such fights; and many, so I hear, have met him, hand to hand, alone in diverse parts of the forest."

"Truly," said the Knight, "the thieving rogue has frightened all the bravery out of Nottinghamshire. Nevertheless, I will do as you bid. A blast from this horn shall tell that he is dead. But come, good Sheriff, we tarry over-long. Rest assured that Robin Hood shall meet his end before the moon cast her beams through the forest leaves."

So the Sheriff gave command, and soon his three hundred stalwart yeoman and foresters stood ready to follow the two leaders, who, both on horseback, rode in front on their way through the forest to destroy the outlaw's nest.

On that very same morning, just before sunrise, you might have seen all of Robin's merry men wrapped snugly in their night-cloaks, fast asleep on the grassy sward, round about the great oak. On a low-hanging branch above Robin's head sat a throstle, singing so loud that it roused him from his sleep. Half raising himself, he looked at the bird, which kept pouring forth its mellow notes and would not cease to sing. Then Robin said:

"Now, last night I had a dream, and it seemed to me that two strong yeoman fought with me fast and furiously. I thought they did beat me and bind me fast to a tree, taking from me both arrows and bow. If I be Robin, and am awake in this merry wood, I will take revenge on those two."

Little John, who lay by his side, had also been awakened by the song-bird and heard what Robin said.

"Dreams are swift, master," said he, "even as the wind that blows o'er the hill. For if it be never so loud this night, tomorrow it may be still enough."

"That is truth," said Robin, "but I shall go to seek these strong yeomen, if they are in the forest."

So he leaped up, and, throwing off his covering, shouted to his comrades: "My merry men, bestir yourselves, and make ready. Little John, you shall go with me."

So they all cast off their cloaks, took up their bows, and, after partaking of a hearty breakfast, stood ready to march wherever their brave captain should direct. And a fine body of men they were—alert, strong, brave, obedient—so Robin and Little John thought, as they strode past in single file away to the green forest.

By the time the sun had risen high in all his glorious splendour, the birds were singing on every spray and twig; the cool morning air was just crisp enough to make walking in the fair forest a delight and put all in a joyous mood. The band had struck a different path under the leadership of Will Scarlet, though ever within sound of Robin's bugle-call as he strode along by the side of Little John. Soon the two came in sight of a tall figure leaning against a tree. He had a long sword and two sharp daggers that he wore by his side, and his body was covered with the hide of a horse, ears, mane, and tail complete.

"God-a-mercy," said Robin, "what is this thing? Is it man or beast?"

"Stand still," said Little John, "under this greenwood tree while I go forth to the strange thing to know what it is."

"Ah, John," said Robin, "I see well you set no store by me. When was I ever wont to send my men before and myself behind? Were it not for the breaking of my bow, John, I would break your head."

These words rankled harshly in John's breast. He spoke not a word in answer, but turned aside and then strode swiftly away to join the main band, leaving Robin standing alone.

He had gone but a short distance when he heard sounds. As he hurried forward, the sounds became shouts and cries, and at last, when he came near, he

beheld a full pitched battle 'twixt the outlaw band and the Sheriff's men. As he rushed along his heart grew sick with heaviness, for he saw two of the band lying dead in a hollow piece of ground by the side of a glade, and in the distance was Will Scarlet, leaping along over rocks and stones for his very life, with the Sheriff and seven score of his men close at his heels.

"One shot now I will shoot," said John, "with all my might and main to make yon Sheriff that presses on so fast stop in his career."

Then he bent his great long-bow and pulled so hard that it burst in twain and the parts fell down at his feet.

"Woe is me," he cried, "wickedest wood, that ever grew on a tree; for now this day when I need you most, you fail me."

The arrow flew, but with such a bad aim that instead of hitting the Sheriff it struck Will-a-Trent to the ground—one of the Sheriff's men who was very friendly with the band. Little John's heart was crushed, and his hands hung limp by his side. Heedless of all that was going on in the fight, he was caught by a number of the Sheriff's men, who took him and quickly bound him to a tree.

When the Sheriff heard that Little John was taken, he came up to where the outlaw was pinioned, to jeer and mock at him.

"I have you now," snarled he. "You shall be drawn up hill and down dale tied to a horse's tail. Then I will hang you from the topmost tower of Nottingham Castle."

"Yet," said Little John, unafraid, "you may fail of your purpose if the good saints have their will. Our men are not all in my situation."

"No," roared the Sheriff, "but Robin Hood is now in the toils of the brave Sir Guy of Gisbourne."

Little John knew of this fell knight, and his heart sank lower than ever to think that Robin was left alone with this villain, whom he now knew to be the creature standing by the tree. So he repented sore that he had crossed his dear master and had left him to his fate.

As soon as Little John had gone, Robin Hood marched up to the man in the horse-hide robe.

"Good morrow, good fellow!" said he.

"Good morrow, good fellow, to you," the other made answer.

"I think by that bow you bear in your hand, you should be a fair archer," said Robin.

"I have lost my way," said the stranger, "and know not where to go."

"I'll lead you good fellow, through the forest and be your guide," said Robin.

"I am seeking for an outlaw," the stranger went on, "that men call Robin Hood, and I would give forty pounds if I could meet with him here."

"Then come along with me, bold fellow, and Robin you shall soon see. But first, under this greenwood tree let us test each other's skill with bow and shaft, for we may meet this Robin Hood by some odd chance in the meantime."

"I like the plan, brave archer," said the stranger; and forthwith they cut a thin sapling that grew among the underbush, which they set in the ground, with a little garland on the top, threescore rods away.

"Lead on, good fellow," said Robin, "and shoot."

"Nay, by my faith, good fellow," said the other, "you shall shoot first."

"Well, so be it," said Robin; "I will do as you say."

The first time Robin shot he missed the wand by an inch; and the stranger, though a right good archer, shot a foot or more away. But upon the

second trial he placed the arrow inside the garland. Then Robin, as he had done many times before, loosed a shaft that cut the wand in two.

"A blessing upon your heart," said the stranger. "Fellow, that shooting is good; and if your heart be as good as your hand, Robin Hood could do no better. Now tell me your name, brave archer."

"No, by my faith," said bold Robin, "that will I not do till you have told me yours."

"I dwell," said he, "upon the moorlands of Yorkshire, and when I am called by my right name, men call me Sir Guy of Gisbourne."

"My dwelling," slowly said Robin, "is in this very wood, and men know me as Robin Hood."

Then, with his hand upon the hilt of his sword, Sir Guy roared out: "You are he whom I have long sought."

"Well," said Robin, "I am ready. Prepare yourself, for with my good broadsword will I cut short your evil life."

Robin drew his sword, and Sir Guy his, at the same time unsheathing his long, pointed Irish dagger, which he held in his left hand. Facing each other with keen eyes, they watched their chance. Both knew the combat was to be long and fierce; both were equally determined to win. Each found the other a worthy foe, for in skill and hardihood they were well matched. No one was by to see fair play, save the birds, and they were soon scared away by the noise of the clashing swords and the deep, angry oaths of the fell Sir Guy, as he fiercely lunged, parried, and feinted. Robin was well aware of the peril in which he stood. Sir Guy was fighting for a great prize. The victor would live, the vanquished would surely die. It was a grim battle to the death.

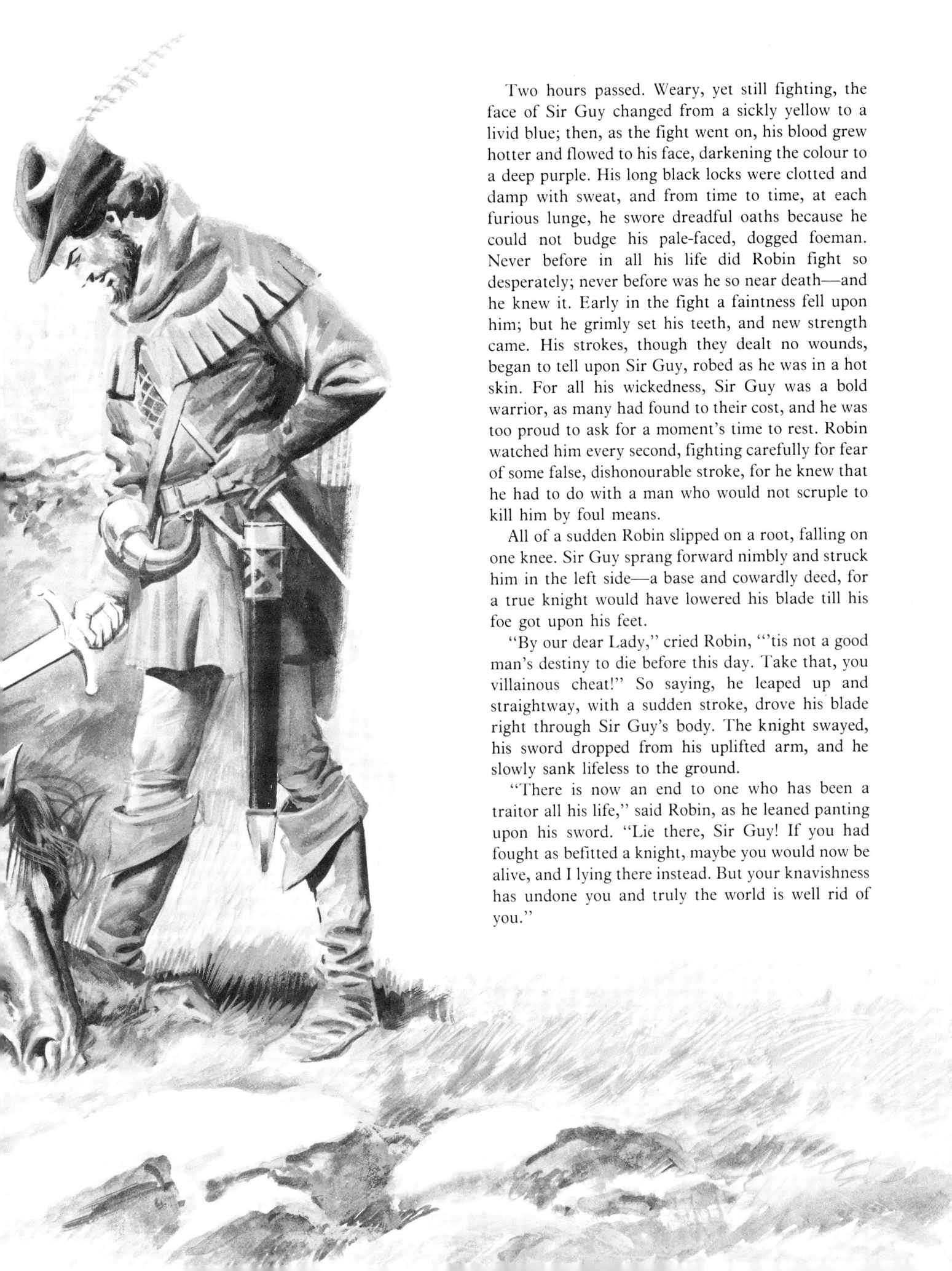

Two hours passed. Weary, yet still fighting, the face of Sir Guy changed from a sickly yellow to a livid blue; then, as the fight went on, his blood grew hotter and flowed to his face, darkening the colour to a deep purple. His long black locks were clotted and damp with sweat, and from time to time, at each furious lunge, he swore dreadful oaths because he could not budge his pale-faced, dogged foeman. Never before in all his life did Robin fight so desperately; never before was he so near death—and he knew it. Early in the fight a faintness fell upon him; but he grimly set his teeth, and new strength came. His strokes, though they dealt no wounds, began to tell upon Sir Guy, robed as he was in a hot skin. For all his wickedness, Sir Guy was a bold warrior, as many had found to their cost, and he was too proud to ask for a moment's time to rest. Robin watched him every second, fighting carefully for fear of some false, dishonourable stroke, for he knew that he had to do with a man who would not scruple to kill him by foul means.

All of a sudden Robin slipped on a root, falling on one knee. Sir Guy sprang forward nimbly and struck him in the left side—a base and cowardly deed, for a true knight would have lowered his blade till his foe got upon his feet.

"By our dear Lady," cried Robin, "'tis not a good man's destiny to die before this day. Take that, you villainous cheat!" So saying, he leaped up and straightway, with a sudden stroke, drove his blade right through Sir Guy's body. The knight swayed, his sword dropped from his uplifted arm, and he slowly sank lifeless to the ground.

"There is now an end to one who has been a traitor all his life," said Robin, as he leaned panting upon his sword. "Lie there, Sir Guy! If you had fought as befitted a knight, maybe you would now be alive, and I lying there instead. But your knavishness has undone you and truly the world is well rid of you."

Robin's wound was but a scratch, for he had partly turned the blow. When he had bound it up and rested a little, he doffed his coat of Lincoln green, and clad himself from top to toe in the horse-hide, saying, "Now I will see how my men have fared and what has befallen Little John." Then he put Sir Guy's horn to his lips and blew so loud a blast that the Sheriff heard it as he stood upon a little hill waiting for the welcome sound.

"Hearken," said the Sheriff, "for I hear good tidings. Yonder I hear Sir Guy blowing his horn, as he said he would do when he had slain Robin Hood. Ay, by the mass, yonder comes the good knight, clad in his horse-hide coat. Come hither, come hither to me, good Sir Guy. Ask whatever you will of me!"

"Oh, I will have none of your gold," said Robin, "nor do I crave any reward save only this: now that I have slain the master, let me go and strike down the knavish servant at yonder tree. No other fee will I have."

"You are a madman," said the Sheriff, "and are truly unworthy of a knight's fee." But he pressed him no further, thinking so large a sum were as well in his own pocket. So he granted Robin's request, though in his heart he longed to carry Little John back to Nottingham alive, as his own prisoner.

When Little John heard his master's voice he knew his freedom was close at hand through some good hap, and now he saw Robin coming as fast as he could hie to cut his bonds. The Sheriff and his men followed close upon Robin's heels to witness the end of Little John.

"Stand aback, stand aback," shouted Robin. "Why do you draw so near? It is not the custom in my country for more than one to hear a man's last confession. Put some space between us, while I do this deed."

So then the men backed away; and Robin, pulling forth the Irish knife, quickly loosed the bonds that held Little John's hands and feet. Then, giving him

Sir Guy's bow and arrows, he bade him look to himself. Both turned about at the same instant with bows ready bent; and when the Sheriff saw that his prisoner was free, he knew that Robin Hood had again foiled his plans. The shock was so great that he had no heart to stand and brave it out, but turned aside and made all haste to ride toward his home in Nottingham town. He fled fast, and all his company did likewise, for they knew the deadly aim of those two archers who had so just a cause for anger against them. But before the Sheriff could ride out of sight Little John shot an arrow which wounded him in the shoulder. Thus he rode into Nottingham town with the broad arrow sticking from his back.

Then it was that Little John turned to Robin, saying: "My dear good master, I do freely ask your pardon, and should you grant it me I make a vow nevermore to cross your will or leave you again in the lurch."

"No, no, my trusty John, my best of true hearts, 'tis I should ask pardon of you, for I was out of temper and hasty of speech I spoke unkindly."

Thereupon they embraced, then through the forest these two firm friends of over a quarter of a century strode together, in quiet happiness, back home to their trysting-place, where they found most of their comrades safe and happy. So the night was spent in feasting and tales of deeds nobly done on that famous day when Sir Guy of Gisbourne was slain.

The Return of King Richard

For long months, King Richard the Lion-hearted had been held a prisoner in Germany. At home, his evil brother John oppressed the unhappy people, and conspired treacherously with certain of the barons for Richard's ruin. At last the king was ransomed by his loyal subjects, and suddenly he was home again. Then all who had oppressed the people or followed the traitor John had to scurry about and cover up the tracks of their misdoings.

Now the Sheriff of Nottingham and the abbot of St Mary's had evil tracks enough to cover up, and it occurred to them that a fine way to do it would be to bring King Richard report of the lawless deeds of the outlaw Robin Hood and all his band. It would be easy indeed, thought they, to hide from the King the fact that Robin's men, whatever their crimes, had always stood out against the cruel Prince John and had been loyal to the absent king. Very persuasive they were, and many were the stories they told the King of Robin's supposed treachery.

But King Richard, wary and bold, determined to see for himself. Disguised as an abbot, he rode alone into the forest.

He had not gone far when, sure enough, he fell among Robin's men, who of course did not know him and made him prisoner and hurried him off to their camp in the depths of Sherwood Forest. There they intended to banquet him courteously, as was their wont with any unfortunate churchman who fell into their hands, and to set him free again—robbed of all his gold. So:

Robin took the king's horse
   Hastily in that stead,
And said, Sir Abbot, by your leave
   A while you must abide.

We be yeomen of this Forest,
   Under the greenwood tree
We live by our king's deer,
   Other shift have not we.

And you have churches and rents both
   And gold full great plenty.
Give me some of your spending
   For Saint Charity.

But the false abbot pleaded that he had no more than forty pounds; for the king, he said was staying with him, and he found it very expensive. Robin took

73

the money and distributed half of it among his men. Then he returned the other half to the king.

"Now, indeed," said the seeming abbot, "let me tell you, bold outlaw, that I have a letter for you from the king himself, commanding you to come to him at Nottingham!"

"The king! King Richard! God and the holy saints bless him!" cried Robin Hood eagerly. "The king is come to right the wrongs Prince John has done! Come, my merry men all, a rousing cheer for King Richard!" And they gave it with a will.

"What are you cheering about?" And there came into their midst a lovely maiden, all clothed in brown and gold to match the autumn woodland.

" 'Tis that the king's come home again, sweet Maid Marian!" said Robin. "This worthy abbot brings good news—better news than he supposed. For I love no man in all the world as I love my king!"

"Nor I," said Maid Marian archly, "save only you, Robin Hood, king of the forest!"

The King at the Feast

You may well imagine that King Richard was amazed at all he heard and saw, and that he eagerly accepted Robin's invitation to feast with them, to see good sport of archery and strong buffeting.

The king played his part as a merry abbot well enough, but he could not help showing unusual strength in buffeting—for Richard was a mighty warrior, as everybody knows, gigantic of stature and great in strength.

"Ha! ha!" cried Maid Marian roguishly, when she saw that the strange abbot had buffeted Robin Hood to his knees. "It gladdens me to see you bow before an abbot!"

Then it was that Richard threw off his abbot's mantle, and stood forth for all to see.

"The king!" exclaimed Robin, falling on one knee —this time without need of buffeting.

"The king!" breathed Maid Marian, and she knelt by Robin's side.

"The king!" shouted all the rest, and bowed themselves.

King Richard was heartily enjoying his jest, and he was thankful enough for the loyalty of bold Robin Hood and his band at a time when his kingdom was rent with quarrels because of Prince John's treachery. So he forgave them all and bade them be outlaws no longer. His only condition was that they should leave the forest and the hunting of the king's deer, and serve him faithfully at his court.

"And this maiden, Sir King?" asked Robin Hood, taking Maid Marian's hand. "She has steadily refused to wed me until the king returns."

"The king has come home now!" cried Richard gaily, "and a wedding feast will be to the liking of us all. Afterwards your wife shall grace the court among the best."

Robin Hood Leaves Sherwood Forest

So Sherwood rang no more with the shouts of the merry men, and Robin and Maid Marian were married and lived happily at the court of the king.

But in time bold Robin grew weary of the court. King Richard died, and King John was a bitter enemy. Maid Marian too was dead, and the days weighed heavily on Robin's heart. At last he was taken so suddenly and violently ill that he knocked at the door of the nunnery of Kirklees, and implored the nuns to bleed him, so that he might recover.

Some say it was the abbess who cut Robin's vein, some say a nun, some say a friar. Whoever it was, instead of binding up the wound, left Robin bleeding, and locked the door on him.

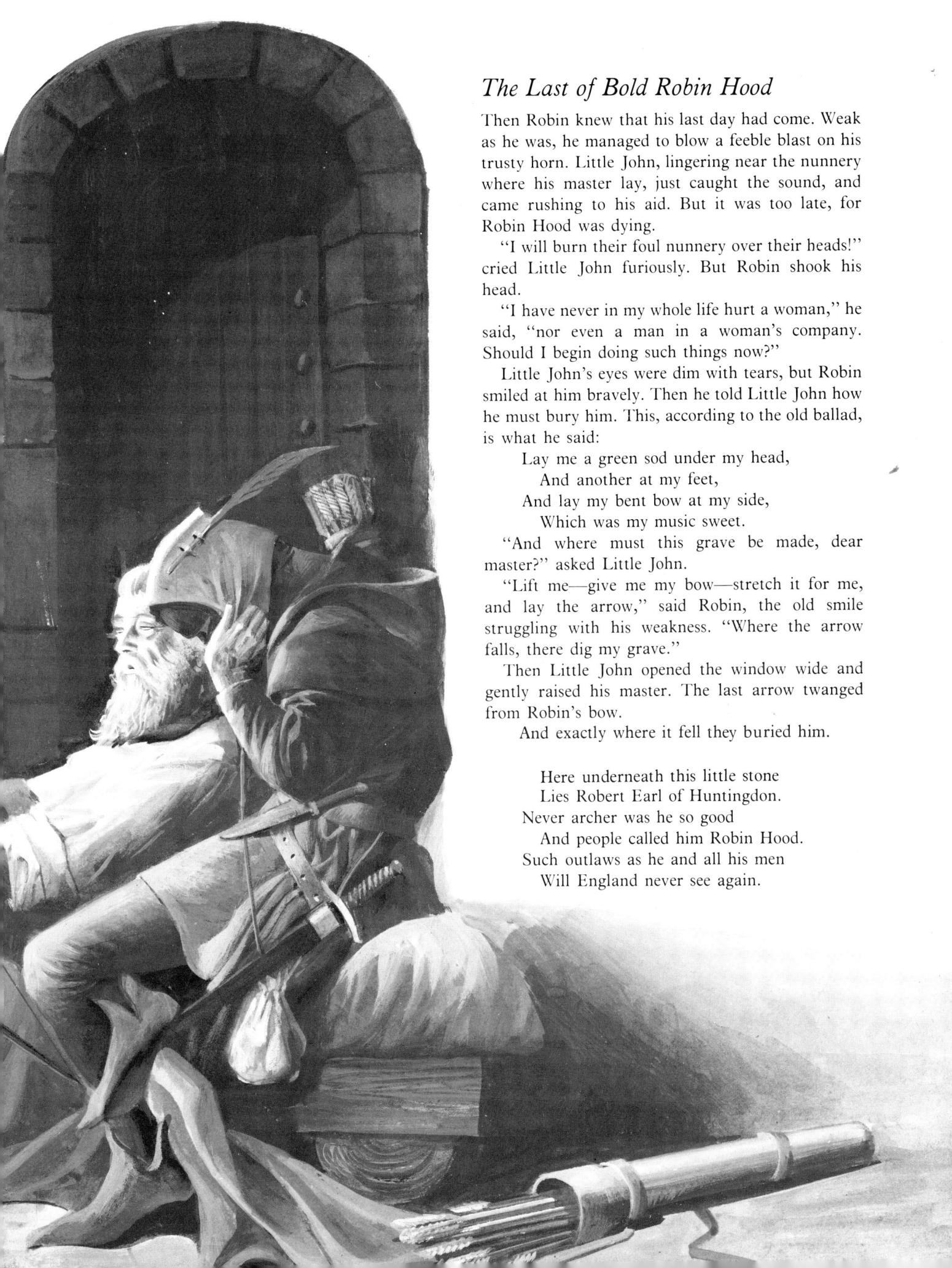

The Last of Bold Robin Hood

Then Robin knew that his last day had come. Weak as he was, he managed to blow a feeble blast on his trusty horn. Little John, lingering near the nunnery where his master lay, just caught the sound, and came rushing to his aid. But it was too late, for Robin Hood was dying.

"I will burn their foul nunnery over their heads!" cried Little John furiously. But Robin shook his head.

"I have never in my whole life hurt a woman," he said, "nor even a man in a woman's company. Should I begin doing such things now?"

Little John's eyes were dim with tears, but Robin smiled at him bravely. Then he told Little John how he must bury him. This, according to the old ballad, is what he said:

> Lay me a green sod under my head,
>> And another at my feet,
> And lay my bent bow at my side,
>> Which was my music sweet.

"And where must this grave be made, dear master?" asked Little John.

"Lift me—give me my bow—stretch it for me, and lay the arrow," said Robin, the old smile struggling with his weakness. "Where the arrow falls, there dig my grave."

Then Little John opened the window wide and gently raised his master. The last arrow twanged from Robin's bow.

And exactly where it fell they buried him.

> Here underneath this little stone
> Lies Robert Earl of Huntingdon.
> Never archer was he so good
>> And people called him Robin Hood.
> Such outlaws as he and all his men
>> Will England never see again.